NIGHTMARE PLANET

NIGHTMARE PLANET

by Murray Leinster

The Directory-ship *Tethys* made the first landing on the planet, L216[12]. It was a goodly world, with an ample atmosphere and many seas, which the nearby sun warmed so lavishly that a perpetual cloud-bank hid them and all the solid ground from view. It had mountains and islands and high plateaus. It had day and night and rain. It had an equable climate, rather on the tropical side. But it possessed no life.

No animals roamed its solid surface. No vegetation grew from its rocks. Not even bacteria struggled with the stones to turn them into soil. No living thing, however small, swam in its oceans. It was one of that disappointing vast majority of otherwise admirable worlds which was unsuited for colonization solely because it had not been colonized before. It could be used for biological experiments in a completely germ-free environment, or ships could land upon it for water and supplies of air. The water was pure and the air breathable, but it had no other present utility. Such was the case with an overwhelming number of Earth-type planets when first discovered in the exploration of the galaxy. Life simply hadn't started there.

So the ship which first landed upon it made due note for the Galactic Directory and went away, and no other ship came near the planet for eight hundred years.

But nearly a millennium later, the Seed-Ship *Orana* arrived. It landed and carefully seeded the useless world. It circled endlessly above the clouds, dribbling out a fine dust comprised of the spores of every conceivable microorganism that could break down rock to powder and turn the powder to organic matter. It also seeded with moulds and fungi and lichens, and everything that could turn powdery primitive soil into stuff on which higher forms of life could grow. The *Orana* seeded the seas with plankton. Then it, too, went away.

Centuries passed. Then the Ecological Preparation Ship *Ludred* swam to the planet from space. It was a gigantic ship of highly improbable construction and purpose. It found the previous seeding successful. Now there was soil which swarmed with minute living things. There were fungi which throve monstrously. The seas stank of teeming minuscule life-forms. There were even some novelties on land, developed by strictly local conditions. There were, for example, *paramecium* as big as grapes, and yeasts had increased in size so that they bore flowers visible to the naked eye. The life on the planet was not aboriginal, though. It had all been planted by the seed-ship of centuries before.

The *Ludred* released insects, it dumped fish into the seas. It scattered plant-seeds over the continents. It treated the planet to a sort of Russell's Mixture of living things. The real Russell's Mixture is that blend of simple elements in the proportions found in suns. This was a blend of living creatures, of whom some should certainly survive by consuming the now habituated flora, and others which should survive by preying on the first. The planet was stocked, in effect, with everything it could be hoped might live there.

But at the time of the *Ludred's* visit of course no creature needing parental care had any chance of survival. Everything had to be able to care for itself the instant it burst its egg. So there were no birds or mammals. Trees and plants of divers sorts, and fish and crustaceans and insects could be planted. Nothing else.

The *Ludred* swam away through emptiness.

There should have been another planting, centuries later still, but it was never made. When the Ecological Preparation Service was moved to Algol IV, a file was upset. The cards in it were picked up and replaced, but one was missed. So that planet was forgotten. It circled its sun in emptiness. Cloud-banks covered it from pole to pole. There were hazy markings in certain places, where high plateaus penetrated the clouds. But from space the planet was featureless. Seen from afar, it was merely a round white ball—white from its cloud-banks and nothing else.

But on its surface, in its lowlands it was nightmare.

Especially was it nightmare—after some centuries—for the descendants of the human beings from the space-liner *Icarus*, wrecked there some forty-odd generations ago. Naturally, nobody anywhere else thought of the *Icarus* any more. It was not even remembered by the descendants of its human cargo, who now inhabited the planet. The wreckage of the ship was long since hidden under the seething, furiously striving fungi of the boil. The human beings on the planet had forgotten not only the ship but very nearly everything—how they came to this world, the use of metals, the existence of fire, and even the fact that there was such a thing as sunlight. They lived in the lowlands, deep under the cloud-bank, amid surroundings which were riotous, swarming, frenzied horror. They had become savages. They were less than savages. They had forgotten their high destiny as men.

*

Dawn came. Grayness appeared overhead and increased. That was all. The sky was a blank, colorless pall, merely mottled where the clouds clustered a little thicker or a little thinner, as clouds do. But the landscape was variegated enough! Where the little group of people huddled together, there was a wide valley. Its walls rose up and up into the very clouds. The people had never climbed those hillsides.

They had not even traditions of what might lie above them, and their lives had been much too occupied to allow of speculations on cosmology. By day they were utterly absorbed in two problems which filled every waking minute. One was the securing of food to eat, under the conditions of the second problem, which was that of merely staying alive.

There was only one of their number who sometimes thought of other matters, and he did so because he had become lost from his group of humans once, and had found his way back to it. His name was Burl, and his becoming lost was pure fantastic accident, and his utilization of a fully inherited power to think was the result of extraordinary events. But he still had not the actual habit of thinking. This morning he was like his fellows.

All of them were soaked with wetness. During the night—every night—the sky dripped slow, spaced, solemn water-drops during the whole of the dark hours. This was customary. But normally the humans hid in the mushroom-forests, sheltered by the toadstools which now grew to three man-heights. They denned in small openings in the tangled mass of parasitic growths which flourished in such thickets. But this last night they had camped in the open. They had no proper habitations of their own. Caves would have been desirable, but insects made use of caves, and the descendants of insects introduced untold centuries before had shared in the size-increase of *paramecium*and yeasts and the few true plants which had been able to hold their own. Mining-wasps were two yards long, and bumble-bees were nearly as huge, and there were other armored monstrosities which also preferred caves for their own purposes. And of course the humans could not build habitations, because anything men built to serve the purpose of a cave would instantly be preempted by creatures who would automatically destroy any previous occupants.

7

NIGHTMARE PLANET

The humans had no fixed dens at any time. Now they had not even shelter. They lacked other things, also. They had no tools save salvaged scraps of insect-armor—great sawtoothed mandibles or razor-pointed leg-shells—which they used to pry apart the edible fungi on which they lived, or to get at the morsels of meat left behind when the brainless lords of this planet devoured each other. They had not even any useful knowledge, except desperately accurate special knowledge of the manners and customs of the insects they could not defy. And on this special morning they concluded that they were doomed. They were going to be killed. They stood shivering in the open, waiting for it to happen.

It was not exactly news. They had had warning days ago, but they could do nothing about it. Their home valley, to be sure, would have made any civilized human being shudder merely to look at it, but they had considered it almost paradise. It was many miles long, and a fair number wide, and a stream ran down its middle. At the lower end of the valley there was a vast swamp, from which at nightfall the thunderously deep-bass croaking of giant frogs could be heard. But that swamp had kept out the more terrifying creatures of that world. The thirty-foot centipedes could not cross it or did not choose to. The mastodon-sized tarantulas which ravaged so much of the planet would not cross it save in pursuit of prey. So the valley was nearly a haven of safety.

True, there was one clotho spider in its ogre's castle nearby, and there was a labyrinth spider in a minor valley which nobody had ever ventured into, and there were some—not many—praying-mantises as tall as giraffes. They wandered terribly here and there. But most members of insect life here were absorbed in their own affairs and ignored the humans. There was an ant-city, whose foot-long warriors competed with the humans as scavengers. There were the bees, trying to eke out a livelihood from the great, cruciform flowers of the giant cabbage-plants and the milkweeds when water-lilies in the swamps did not bear their four-foot blooms. Wasps sought their own prey. Flies were consumers of corruption, but even the flies two feet in length would shy away from a man who waved his arms at it. So this valley had seemed to these people to be a truly admirable place.

But a fiend had entered it. As the gray light grew stronger the shivering folk looked terrifiedly about them. There were only twenty of the people now. Two weeks before there had been thirty. In a matter of days or less, there would be none. Because the valley had been invaded by a great gray furry spider!

*

There was a stirring, not far from where the man-folk trembled. Small, inquisitive antennae popped into view among a mass of large-sized pebbles. There was a violent stirring, and gravel disappeared. Small black things thrust upward into view and scurried anxiously about. They returned to the spot from which they had emerged. They were ants, opening the shaft of their city after scouting for danger outside. They scratched and pulled and tugged at the plug of stones. They opened the ant-city's artery of commerce. Strings of small black things came pouring out. They averaged a foot in length, and they marched off in groups upon their divers errands. Presently a group of huge-jawed soldier-ants appeared, picking their way stolidly out of the opening. They waited stupidly for the workers they were to guard. The workers came, each carrying a faintly greenish blob of living matter. The caravan moved off. The humans knew exactly what it was. The green blobs were aphids—plant lice: ant-cows—small creatures sheltered and guarded by the ants and daily carried to nearby vegetation to feed upon its sap and yield inestimable honeydew.

Something reared up two hundred yards away, where the thin mist that lay everywhere just barely began to fade all colorings before it dimmed all outlines. The object was slender. It had a curiously humanlike head. It held out horrible sawtoothed arms in a gesture as of benediction—which was purest mockery. Something smaller was drawing near to it. The colossal praying mantis held its pose, immovable. Presently it struck downward with lightning speed. There was a cry. The mantis rose erect again, its great arms holding something that stirred and struggled helplessly, and repented its unconsonanted outcry. The mantis ate it daintily as it struggled and screamed.

The humans did not watch this tragedy. The mantis would eat a man, of course. It had. The only creatures immune to its menace were ants, which for some reason it would not touch. But it was a mantis' custom after spotting its prey to wait immobile for the unlucky creature to come within its reach. It preferred to make its captures that way. Only if a thing fled did the mantis pursue with deadly ferocity. Even then it dined with monstrous deliberation as this one dined now. Still, mantises could be seen from a

9

distance and hidden from. They were not the terror which had driven the humans even from their hiding-places.

It had been two weeks since the giant hunting-spider had come through a mountain pass into this valley to prey upon the life within it. It was gigantic even of its kind. It was deadliness beyond compare. The first human to see it froze in terror. It was disaster itself. Its legs spanned yards. Its fangs were needle-sharp and feet in length—and poisoned. Its eyes glittered with insatiable, insane blood-lust. Its coming was ten times more deadly to the unarmed folk than a Bengal tiger loose in the valley would have been.

It killed a man the very first day it was in the valley, leaving his sucked-dry carcass, and going on to destroy a rhinoceros-beetle and a cricket—whose deep-bass cries were horrible—and proceeded down the valley, leaving only death behind it. It had killed other men and women since. It had caught four children. But even that was not the worst. It carried worse, more deadly, more inevitable disaster with it.

Because, bumping and bouncing behind its abdomen as it moved, fastened to its body with cables of coarse and discolored silk, the hunting-spider dragged a burden which was its own ferocity many times multiplied. It dragged an egg-bag. The bag was larger than its body, four feet in diameter. The female spider would carry this burden—cherishing it—until the eggs hatched. Then there would be four to five hundred small monsters at large in the valley. And from the instant of their hatching they would be just such demoniac creatures as their parents. They would be small, to be sure. Their legs would span no more than a foot. Their bodies would be the size of a man's fist. But they could leap two yards, instantly they reached the open air, and their inch-long fangs would be no less envenomed, and their ferocity would be in madness, in insanity and in stark maniacal horror equal the great gray fiend which had begot them.

The eggs had hatched. Today—now—this morning—they were abroad. The little group of humans no longer hid in the mushroom-forests because the small hunting-spiders sought frenziedly there for things to kill. Hundreds of small lunatic demons roamed the valley. They swarmed among the huge toadstools, killing and devouring all living things large and small. When they encountered each other they fought in slavering, panting fury, and the survivors of such duels dined upon their brothers. Small truffle-beetles died, clicking futilely. Infinitesimal grubs, newly hatched from butterfly eggs and barely six inches long, furnished them with tidbits. But they would kill anything and feast upon it.

A woman had died yesterday, and two small gray devils battled murderously above her corpse.

Just before darkness a huge yellow butterfly had flung itself agonizedly aloft, with these small dark horrors clinging to its body, feasting upon the juices of the body their poison had not yet done to death.

And now, at daybreak, the humans looked about despairingly for their own deaths to come to them. They had spent the night in the open lest they be trapped in the very forests that had been their protection. Now they remained in clear view of the large gray murderer should it pass that way. They did not dare to hide because of that ogreish creature's young, who panted in their blood-lust as they scurried here and there and everywhere.

As the day became established, the clouds were gray—gray only. The night-mist thinned. One of the younger women of the tribe—a girl called Saya—saw the huge thing far away. She cried out, choking. The others saw the monster as it leaped upon and murdered a vividly colored caterpillar on a milkweed near the limit of vision. The milkweed was the size of a tree. The caterpillar was four yards long. While the enormous victim writhed as it died, not one of the humans looked away. Presently all was still. The hunting-spider crouched over its victim in obscene absorption. Having been madness incarnate, it now was the very exemplar of a horrid gluttony.

Again the humans shivered. They were without shelter. They were without even the concept of arms. But it was morning, and they were alive, and therefore they were hungry. Their desperation was absolute, but desperation to some degree was part of their lives. Yet they shivered and suffered. There were edible mushrooms nearby, but with the deadly small replicas of the hunting-spider giant roaming everywhere, any movement was as likely to be deadly as standing still to be found and killed. The humans murmured to one another, fearfully.

But there was the young man called Burl, who had been lost from his tribe and had found it again. The experience had changed him. He had felt stirrings of atavistic impulses in recent weeks—the more especially when the young girl Saya looked at him. It was not normal, in humans

11

conditioned to survive by flight, that Burl should feel previously unimagined hunger for fury—a longing to hate and do battle. Of course men sometimes fought for a particular woman's favor, but not when there were deadly insects about. The carnivorous insects were not only peril, but horror unfaceable. So Burl's sensations were very strange. On this planet a courtship did not usually involve displays of valor. A man who was a more skillful forager than the foot-long ants was an acceptable husband. Warriors did not exist.

Burl did not even know what a warrior was. Yet today the sullen, unreasonable impulses to conduct what he could not quite imagine were very strong. He knew all the despairing terror the others felt. But he also was hungry. The sheer doom that was upon his group did not change the fact that he wanted to eat, nor did it change the fact that he felt queer when the girl Saya looked at him. Because she was terrified, the same sort of atavistic process was at work in her. She looked to Burl. Men no longer served as protectors against enemies so irresistible as giant spiders. It was not possible. But when Burl realized her regard his chest swelled. He felt a half-formed impulse to beat upon it. His new-found reasoning processes told him that this particular fear was different in some fashion from the terrors men normally experienced. It was. This was a different sort of emergency. Most dangers were sudden and either immediately fatal or somehow avoidable. This was different. There was time to savor its meaning and its hopelessness. It seemed as if it should be possible to do something about it. But Burl was not able, as yet, to think what to do. The bare idea of doing anything was unusual, now. Because of it, though, Burl was able to disregard his terror when Saya regarded him yearningly.

*

The other men muttered to each other of the sudden death in the mushroom thickets. No less certain death now feasted on the dead yellow caterpillar. But Burl abruptly pushed his way clear of the small crowd and scowled for Saya to see. He moved toward the nearest fungus-thicket. An edible mushroom grew at its very edge. He marched toward it, swaggering. Men did not often swagger on this planet.

But then he ceased to swagger. His approach to the mingled mass of toadstools and lesser monstrosities grew slower. His feet dragged. He came to a halt. His impulse to combat conflicted with the facts of here and now.

His flesh crawled at the thought of the grisly small beasts which now might be within yards. These thickets had been men's safest hiding-places. Now they were places of surest disaster.

He stopped, with a coldness at the pit of his stomach. But as it was a new experience to be able to have danger come in a form which could be foreseen, so Burl now had a new experience in that he was ashamed to be afraid. Somehow, having tacitly undertaken to get food for his companions, he could not bring himself to draw back while they watched. But he did want desperately to get the food in a hurry and get away from there.

He saw a gruesome fragment of a tragedy of days before. It was the emptied, scraped, hollow leg-shell of a beetle. It was horrendously barbed. Great, knife-edged spines lined its edge. They were six inches in length. And men did not have weapons any more, but they sometimes used just such objects as this to dismember defenseless giant slugs they came upon.

Burl picked up the hollow shell of the leg-joint. He shook it free of clinging moulds—and small things an inch or two in length dropped from it and scurried frantically into hiding. He moved hesitantly toward the edible mushroom which would be food for Saya and the rest. He was four yards from the thicket. Three. Two. He needed to move only six feet, and then slice at the flabby mushroom-head, and he would be at least an admirable person in the eyes of Saya.

Then he cried out thinly. Something small, with insane eyes, leaped upon him from the edge of a giant toadstool.

It was, of course, one of the small beasts which had hatched from the hunting-spider's egg-bag. It had grown. Its legs now spanned sixteen inches. Its body was as large as Burl's two fists together. It was big enough to enclose his head in a cage of loathesomeness formed by its legs, while its fangs tore at his scalp. Or it could cover his chest with its abominableness while its poison filled his veins, and while it feasted upon him afterward....

He flung up his hands in a paralytic, horror-stricken attempt to ward it off. But they were clenched. His right hand did not let go of the leg-section with its razor-sharp barbs.

The spider struck the beetle-leg. He felt the impact. Then he heard gaspings and bubblings of fury. He heard an indescribable cry which was madness itself. The chitinous object he had picked up now shook and quivered of itself.

13

NIGHTMARE PLANET

The spider was impaled. Two of its legs were severed and twitched upon the ground before him. Its body was slashed nearly in half. It writhed and struggled and made beastly sounds. Thin, colored fluids dripped from it. A disgusting musky smell filled the air. It strove to reach and kill him as it died. Its eyes looked like flames.

Burl's arm shook convulsively. The small thing dropped to the ground. Its remaining legs moved frantically but without purpose.

It died, though its leg continued to twitch and stir and quiver.

Burl remained frozen, for seconds. It was an acquired instinct; a conditioned reflex which humans had to develop on this world. When danger was past, one stayed desperately still lest it return. But Burl's thoughts were now not of horror but a vast astonishment. He had killed a spider! He had killed a thing which would have killed him! He was still alive!

And then, being a savage, and an animal, as well as a human being, he acted according to that highly complicated nature. As a savage, he knew with strict practicality that it was improbable that there was another baby spider nearby. If there had been, they would have fought each other. As an animal, he was again hungry. As a human being, he was vain.

So he moved closer to the toadstool-thicket and put his hand out and broke off a great mass of the one edible mushroom at the edge. A noisesome broth poured out and little maggots dropped to the ground and writhed there in it. But most of what he had broken off was sound. He turned to take it to Saya. Then he saw the dropped weapon and the spider. He picked up the weapon.

The spider's legs still twitched, though futilely. He spiked the small body on the beetle-leg's spines. He strode back to the remnant of his tribe with a peculiar gait that even he had not often practiced.

It was rather more pronounced than a swagger. It was a strut.

They trembled when they saw the dead creature he had killed. He gave Saya the food. She took it, looking at him with bright and intense eyes. He took a part of the mushroom for himself and ate it, scowling. Thoughts were struggling to form in his mind. He was not accustomed to thinking, but he had done more of it than any other of the pitiful group about him.

He felt eyes watching him. There were five adult men in this group besides himself, and six women. The rest were children, from gangling

14

adolescents to one mere infant in arms. They were a remarkably colorful group at the moment, had he only known it. The men wore yellow-and-gold-brown loin-cloths of caterpillar-fur, stripped from the drained carcasses of creatures that the formerly resident clothed spider had killed. The women wore cloaks of butterfly-wing, similarly salvaged from the remnants of a meal left unfinished by a finicky or engorged praying mantis. The stuff was thick and leathery, but it was magnificently tinted in purples and yellows.

Time passed. The mushroom Burl had brought was finished. Some eyes always explored the clear ground around this group. But other eyes fixed themselves upon Burl. It was not a consciously questioning gaze. It was surely not a hopeful one. But men and women and children looked at him. They marveled at him. He had dared to go and get food! He had been attacked by one of the creatures who doomed them all, but he was not dead! Instead, he had killed the spider! It was marvelous! It was unparalleled that a man should kill anything that attacked him!

*

The doomed small group regarded Burl with wondering eyes. He brushed his hands together. He looked at Saya. He wished to be alone with her. He wished to know what she thought when she looked at him. Why she looked at him. What she felt when she looked at him.

He stood up and said dourly:

"Come!"

She moved timidly and gave him her hand. He moved away. There was but one way that any human being on this planet would think to move, from this particular spot just now—away from the still-feasting gigantic horror whose offspring he had killed. The folk shivered near the edge of the first upward slope of the valley wall. Burl moved in that direction. Toward the slope. Saya went with him.

Before they had gone ten yards a man spoke to his wife. They followed Burl, with their three children. Five yards more, and two of the remaining three adult men were hustling their families in his wake also. In seconds the last was in motion.

Burl moved on, unconscious of any who followed him, aware only of Saya. The procession, absurd as it was, continued in his wake simply because it had begun to do so. A skinny, half-grown boy regarded Burl's stained weapon. He saw something half-buried in the soil and moved aside to tug at it. It was part of the armor of a former rhinoceros-beetle. He went on, rather awkwardly holding a weapon which might have been called a dagger, eighteen inches long, except that no dagger would have a hand-guard nearly its own length in diameter.

They passed a struggling milkweed plant, no more than twenty feet high and already scabrous with scale and rusts upon its lower parts. Ants marched up and down its stalk in a steady, single file, placing aphids from the ant-city on suitable spots to feed, and to multiply as only parthenogenic aphids can do. But already on the far side of the milkweed, an ant-lion climbed up to do murder among them. The ant-lion was the larval form the lace-wing fly, of course. Aphids were its predestined prey.

Burl continued to march, holding Saya's hand. The reek of formic acid came to his nostrils. But that was only ants. The slope grew steeper. Massacre began behind him on the tree-sized milkweed. The ant-lion which even when it was but half an inch long, on Earth, could bite through the skin of a man—the ant-lion reached the pasturing cows. It plunged into slaughter. It was demoniac. It was such ghastly ferocity that the eggs from which its kind hatched were equipped, each one, with a plastic column to hold it well away from the object on which the clutch of eggs were laid. But for this precaution by the maternal lace-wing fly, the first of her brood to hatch would devour its unhatched brothers and sisters. This ant-lion charged into the placidly feeding aphids on the milkweed plant. It seized one and crushed it, holding it aloft so that the juices of its body would pour into the ant-lion's mouth. Almost instantly, it seemed, the mild-eyed aphid was a shrunken empty sack. The ant-lion seized another. The remaining aphids fed placidly while their enemy did vast slaughter among them.

Clickings and a shrill stridulation sounded. Warrior-ants climbed with stupid ferocity to offer battle.

Burl moved on to a minor eminence. He reached its top and looked sharply about him with the caution that was the price of existence on this world. Two hundred feet away, a small scurrying horror raged and searched among the rough-edged layers of what on other worlds was called paper-mould or rock-tripe. Here it was thick as quilting, and infinitesimal creatures denned under it. The sixteen-inch spider devoured them, making gluttonous sounds. But it was busy, and all spiders are relatively short-sighted.

Burl turned to Saya—and realized that all the human folk had followed him. One of the adults was reaching fearfully for part of a discarded cricket-shell in the ground. He tore free an emptied, sickle-shaped jaw. It was curved and sharp and deadly if properly wielded. The man had seen Burl kill something. He tried vaguely to imagine killing something himself. He was not too successful. Another man tugged at the ground. The skinny boy was practicing thrusts with his giant dagger.

Two of the adults were armed, without any clear idea of what to do with their arms. But Burl knew, now.

He regarded them angrily. He had not meant to desert them, or even to take Saya permanently from among them. Humans had little enough of satisfaction on this planet. The scared company of their kind was one of the most important. So Burl did not resent that they had followed him. He did resent that they were near when he wanted to talk to Saya in what he did not yet think of as lover-like seclusion.

They halted, regarding him humbly. They had been hungry, and he had found food for them. They had been paralyzed by terror, and he had dared to move. So they moved with him. They might have followed anybody else, but only Burl had initiative—so far. They trustfully waited to follow and to imitate him for so long as panic numbed their ability to think for themselves.

Burl opened his mouth to shout furiously at them. But it was not a good idea for humans to draw attention. Spiders did not hunt by scent, but sound sometimes drew them. Burl closed his mouth again, in a taut straight line. The men looked at him supplicatingly. They had never been lost, and so had never learned to think even a little. Burl had learned to think in a rudimentary fashion and now he suddenly perceived that it was pleasing to have all the tribe regard him so worshipfully, even if not in quite the same fashion as Saya. He was suddenly aware that even as Saya had obeyed him when he told her to come with him, they would obey. He had, at the moment, no commands to give, but he immediately invented one for the pleasure of seeing it carried out.

"*I carry sharp things,*" he said sternly. "I killed a spider. Go find *sharp things* to carry."

NIGHTMARE PLANET

They were a meek and abject folk, and they were desperately in need of something to do to take their minds from the uselessness of doing anything at all.

They moved to obey. Saya would have loosened her hand and obeyed, too, but Burl held her beside him. One of the women, with a child three years old, laid the child down by Burl's feet while she went fearfully to seek some fragment of a dead creature, that would meet Burl's specification of sharpness.

Burl heard a stifled scream. A ten-year-old boy stood paralyzed, staring in an agony of horror at something which had stepped from behind a misshapen fungoid object.

It was a pallidly greenish creature with a small head and enormous eyes. It was a very few inches taller than a man. Its abdomen swelled gracefully into a pleasing, leaf-like shape. The boy faced it, paralyzed by horror, and it stood stock-still. Its great, hideously spiny arms were spread out in a pose of pious benediction.

It was a partly-grown praying mantis, not very long hatched. It stood rigid, waiting benignly for the boy to come closer. If he fled, it would fling itself after him with ferocity beside which the fury of a tiger would seem kittenish. If he approached, its fanged arms would flash down, pierce his body, and hold him inextricably fast by the spikes that were worse than trap-claws. And of course it would not wait for him to die before it began its meal.

The small party of humans stood frozen. They were filled with horror for the boy. They were cast into a deep abyss of despair by the sight of a half-grown mantis, because if there was one such miniature insect-dinosaur in the valley, there would be many others. Hundreds of others. This meant there had been a hatching of them. And they were as deadly as spiders.

*

But Burl did not think in such terms just now. Vanity filled him. He had commanded, and he had been obeyed. But now obedience was forgotten because there was this young praying mantis. If men had ever thought of fighting such a creature, it could have destroyed any number of them by pure ferocity and superiority of armament. But Burl raged. He ran toward the spot. Even mantises were sometimes frightened by the unexpected. Burl seized a lumpish object barely protruding from the ground. It looked like

18

a rock. It was actually a flattened ball-fungus, feeding on the soil through thin white threads beneath it. Burl wrenched it free and hurled it furiously at the young monster.

Insects simply do not think. Something came swiftly at it, and the mantis flashed its ghastly arms to seize and kill its attacker. The ball-fungus was heavy. It literally knocked the mantis backward. The boy fled frantically. The insect fought crazily against the thing it thought had assailed it.

The humans gathered around Burl hundreds of yards away—again uphill. The slope of the mountain-flank was marked here. They gathered about Burl because of an example set by the woman who had left her three-year-old child behind. Saya, in the unfailing instinct of a girl for a small child, had snatched it up when Burl left her. Then she had joined him because the instinct which had made her obey him in starting off—it was not quite the same instinct which moved the others—also bade her follow him wherever he went. The mother of the child went to retrieve her deposit. Other figures moved cautiously toward him. The tribe was reconvened.

The floor of the valley seemed a trifle obscured. The mist that hung always in the air made it seem less distinct; less actual; not quite as real as it had been.

Burl gulped and said sternly:

"Where are the sharp things?"

The men looked at one another, numbly. Then one spoke despairingly, ignoring Burl's question. "Now," said the man dully, "there was not only the hunting-spider in the valley, but its young. And not only the young of the hunting-spider, but the young of a mantis ... It was hard to stay alive at the best of times. Now it had become impossible ..."

Burl glared at him. It was neither courage nor resolution. He had come to realize what a splendid sensation it was to be admired by one's fellows. The more he was admired, the better. He was enraged that people thought to despair.

"I," said Burl haughtily, "am *not* going to stay here. I go to a place where there are neither spiders nor mantises. Come!"

He held out his hand to Saya. She gave the child to its mother and took his hand. Burl stalked haughtily away, and she went with him. He went uphill. Naturally. He knew there were spiders and mantises in the valley. So many that to stay there was to die. So he went away from where they were.

Burl had found out that adulation was enjoyable and authority delectable. He had found that it was pleasant to be a dictator. And then he had been disregarded. So he marched furiously away from his folk, in exactly the fashion of a spoiled child refusing to play any longer. He happened to march up the mountainside toward the cloud-bank that he considered the sky. He had no conscious intent to climb the mountain. He did not intend to lead the others. He meant to sulk, by punishing them through the removal of his own admirable person from their society. But they followed him.

So he led his people upward. It has happened on other planets, in other manners. Most human achievements come about through the daring of those who strive.

*

The sun was very near. It shone upon the top of the cloud-bank and the clouds glowed with a marvelous whiteness. It shone upon the mountain-peaks where they penetrated the clouds, and the peaks were warmed, and there was no snow anywhere despite the height. There were winds here where the sun shone. The sky was very blue. At the edge of the plateau where the cloud-bank lay below, the mountainsides seemed to descend into a sea of milk. Great undulations in the mist had the seeming of waves, which moved with great deliberation toward the shores. They seemed sometimes to break against the mountain-wall where it was cliff-like, and sometimes they seemed to flow up gentler inclinations like water flowing up a beach.

All this was in the slowest of slow motion, because the cloud-waves were sometimes miles from crest to crest.

The look of things was different on the plateau, too. This part of the unnamed world, no less than the lowlands, had been seeded with life on two separate occasions. Once with bacteria and moulds and lichens to break up the rocks and make soil of them, and once with seeds and insects-eggs and such living things as might sustain themselves immediately upon hatching. But here on the heights the conditions were drastically unlike the lowland tropic moisture. Different things had thrived, and in quite different fashion.

Here moulds and yeasts and rusts were stunted by the sunlight. Grasses and weeds and trees survived, instead. This was an ideal environment for plants that needed sunlight to form chlorophyll, and chlorophyll to make use of the soil that had been formed. So here was vegetation that was nearly Earth-like. And there was a remarkable side-effect on the fauna which had been introduced at the same time and in the same manner as down below. In coolness which amounted to a temperate climate there could be no such frenzy of life as formed the nightmare-jungles in the lowlands. Plants grew at a slower tempo than fungi, and less luxuriantly. There was no adequate food-supply for large-sized plant-eaters. Insects which were to survive in sunshine could not grow to be monsters. Moreover, the nights were chill. Many insects grow torpid in the cool of a temperate-zone night, but warm up to activity soon after sunrise. But a large creature, made torpid by cold, will not revive so quickly. If large enough, it will not become fully active until close to dusk. On the plateau, the lowland monsters would starve in any case. But more—they would have only a fraction of a day of full activity.

There was a necessary limit then, to the size of the insects that lived above the clouds. The life on the plateau would not have seemed horrifying at all to humans living on other planets. Save for the absence of birds to sing and lack of a variety of small mammals, the untouched sunlit plateau with its warm days and briskly chill nights would have impressed most men as an ideal habitation.

But Burl and his companions were hardly prepared to see it that way at first glimpse. Certainly if told about it beforehand, they would have viewed it with despair.

But they did not know beforehand. They toiled upward, their leader moved by such ridiculous motives as have sometimes caused men to achieve greatness throughout all history. Back on Earth, two great continents were discovered by a man trying to get spices to conceal the gamey flavor of half-spoiled meat. The power that drives mile-long space-craft, and that lights and runs the cities of the galaxy, was first developed because it could be used in bombs to kill other men. There were precedents for Burl leading his fellows into sunshine merely because he was angered that they ceased to admire him.

The trudging, climbing folk were high above the valley, now. The thin mist that was never absent anywhere had hidden their former home, little by little. They climbed a steeply slanting mountain-flank. The stone was mostly covered by ragged, bluish-green rock-tripe in partly overlapping sheets. Such stuff is always close behind the bacteria which first attack a rock-face. On a slope, it clings while soil is washed downward as fast as it forms. The people never ate it. It produced frightening cramps. In time they would learn that if thoroughly dried it can he soaked to pliability again and cooked to a reasonable palatability. But so far they knew neither dryness nor fire.

Nor had they ever known such surroundings as presently enveloped them. A slanting, stony mountainside which stretched up frighteningly to the very sky. Grayness overhead. Grayness, also, to one side—the side away from the mountain. And equal grayness below. The valley in which they lived could no longer be seen at all. Trudging and scrambling up the interminable incline, the people of Burl's personal following gradually realized the strangeness of their surroundings. As one result, they grew sick and dizzy. To them it seemed that the solid earth had tilted, and might presently tilt further. There was no horizon, but they had never seen a horizon. So they felt that what had been *down* was now partly *behind*, and they feared lest a turning universe let them fall ultimately toward the grayness they considered sky.

In this frightening strangeness, their only consolation was the company of their fellows. To stop would be to be abandoned in this place where all values were turned topsy-turvy. To go back—but none of them could imagine descending again to be devoured as one-third of their number already had been. If Burl had stopped, his followers would have squatted down and shivered together miserably, and waited for death. They had no thought of adventure nor any hope of safety. The only goodnesses they could imagine were food and the nearness of other humans. They clung together, obsessed by the dread of being left alone.

Burl's motivation was no longer noble. He had started uphill in a fit of sulks, and he was ashamed to stop.

They came to a place where the mountain-flank sank inward. There was a flat area, and behind it there was a winding cañon of sorts, like a vast crack in the mountain's substance. Burl breasted the curving edge, and walked on level ground. Then he stopped short.

The mouth of the cañon was perhaps fifty yards from the lip of the downward slope. There was this level space, and on it there were toadstools and milkweed, and there was food. It was a small, isolated asylum for life such as they were used to. It could have been that here they could have found safety. But it wasn't that way.

*

They saw the web at once. It was slung from between the opposite cliff-walls by cables two hundred feet long. Its radiating cables reached down to anchorages on stone. The snare-threads, winding out and out in that logarithmic spiral which men on other planets had noted thousands of years before—the snare-threads were a yard apart. The web was set for giant game. It was empty now, but Burl searched keenly and saw the tight-rope-cable leading from the very center of the web to a rocky shelf some fifty feet above the cañon's floor. At its end he saw the spider. It waited there, almost invisible against the stone, with one furry leg touching the cable that led to its waiting-place so that the slightest touch on any part of the web would warn it instantly.

Burl's followers accumulated behind him. They stared. They knew, of course, that a web-spider will not leave its snare under any normal circumstances. They were not afraid of that. But they looked at the ground between the web and themselves.

It was a charnel-house of murdered creatures. Half-inch-thick wing-cases of dead beetles. The cleaned-out carcasses of other giants. The ovipositor of an ichneumon-fly—six feet of slender, springy, deadly-pointed tube—and abdomen-plates of bees and draggled antennae of moths and butterflies.

Something very terrible lived in this small place. The mountainsides were barren of food for big flying things. Anything which did fly so high for any reason would never land on sloping, foodless stone. It would land here. And very obviously it would die. Because something—something—killed them as they came. It denned back in the cañon where they could not see. It dined here.

The humans looked and shivered. All but Burl. He deliberately chose for himself a magnificent lance grown by one dead creature for its own defense. He pulled it out of the ground and cleaned it with his hands. He seemed absorbed, but he was terribly aware of the inner depths of the cañon. He was actually pretending, for the sake of what he believed his dignity.

Fearfully, the other humans imitated him in choosing weapons from the armory of the devoured. Then Burl stalked grandly to one side and began to climb again. His people followed him in numbed silence. They were filled with dread, but it was not quite terror. Insects do not stalk their prey. The deadly unseen monster of the cañon had not attacked them. Therefore, it did not know they were there. And therefore they were safe from it until it appeared. But none of them desired to stay.

The slope lessened here, and half a mile further on there was a small thicket of mushrooms. From within it came the cheerful loud clicking of some small beetle, arrived at this spot nobody could possibly know how, but happily ensconced in a twenty-yard patch of jungle above a hollow that had gathered soil through the centuries. There were edible mushrooms in the thicket.

The humans ate. Naturally. And here they realized that they were no longer doomed by the creatures in the valley. Since their climb began they had seen no dangerous thing except the one gigantic, motionless web-spider. They had left the valley and its particular dangers behind.

A man exclaimed in naïve astonishment. He was eating raw mushroom at the moment, and his mouth was full. But abruptly it occurred to him that their doom was lifted. He mentioned the fact in a sort of startled wonder.

"We will stay here," he added happily. "There is food."

And Burl regarded him with knitted brows. Burl was well on the way to becoming spoiled. He had tasted power over his folk, and he found himself jealous of any decision by anybody else.

"I go on," he said haughtily. "Now! You may stay behind if you wish—alone!"

He broke off food for the journey. He held out his hand to Saya. He went on. And again he went upward because to go back was to go to the cañon of the unknown killer. And his folk docilely followed him. They did not really reason about it. To follow him had become a pattern, more or less precarious. In time it could become a habit. Over a period of years it could even become a tradition.

The procession marched on and up. Burl noticed that the air seemed clearer, here. It was not the misty, quasi-transparent stuff of the valley. He could see for miles to right and left, and the curvatures of the mountain-face. But he could not see the valley.

Then he realized that the cloud-bank he saw was finite—an object. He had never thought of it specifically before. To him it had seemed simply the sky.

Now he saw an indefinite lower surface which yet definitely hid the heights toward which he moved. He and his followers were less than a thousand feet below it. It appeared to Burl that presently he would run into an obstacle that would simply keep him from going any further. But until that happened he obstinately continued to climb.

The thing which was the sky appeared to stir. It moved. A little higher, and he could see that there were parts of it which were lower than he was. They moved also. But they did not approach him. And he had no experience of anything inimical which did not plunge upon its victims. Therefore he was not afraid.

In fact, a little later he observed that the whiteness retreated before him, and he was pleased. Weak things such as humans fled aside when predators approached. Here was something which fled aside at his approach. His followers undoubtedly observed the same phenomenon. He had killed a spider. He was a remarkable person. This unknown white stuff was afraid of him.

Burl, with bland conceit, marched confidently through the cloud-bank, ever climbing. At its thickest, he could see only feet in each direction, but always when he advanced threateningly upon opacity, it cleared before him.

Presently the gray light grew brighter. Burl and his folk were accustomed to a shadowless illumination such as fungi could endure—the equivalent of a heavily overcast day on an Earth-type planet. Now the mist about him took on a luminosity which was of a different kind. Suddenly he noticed the silence. He had never known even comparative silence before in all his life. His ears had been assailed every minute since he had been born by a din which was the noise of creatures. By stridulations, by chirpings, by screams, or at the least by the clicking of armor or the deep-toned pulsations of wings. He had always lived in the uproar of frenzied struggle. Now, that hellish chorus of shrieks and cries and mating-calls was cut off. The lower surface of the cloud-bank reflected it. Burl and his people moved upward through an unparalleled stillness.

They fell silent, marveling. They heard each other's movements. They could hear each other's voices. But they moved in a vast quietness over stones which here were not even lichen-covered, but glistened with wet. And all about them a golden glow hung in the very air. Stillness, and quietude, and golden light which grew stronger and stronger and stronger....

It was very remarkable when they came up through the sea of mist upon a shore of sunshine, and saw blue sky and sunlight for the first time. The light smote upon their pink skins and brilliantly colored furry garments. It glinted in changing, ever-more-colorful flashes upon the cloaks made of butterfly wings. It sparkled upon the great lance carried by Burl in the lead, and the quite preposterous weapons borne by his followers.

The little party of twenty humans waded ashore through the last of the thinning white stuff which was cloud. They gazed about them with blinking, wondering, astounded eyes. The sky was blue. There was green grass. And there was sound. The sound was of wind blowing in the trees and sunshine.

They heard insects, too, but they did not know what it was they heard. The shrill, small musical whirrings, the high-pitched small cries which made up a strange new elfin melody, were totally strange. All things were novel to their eyes, and an enormous exultation filled them. From deep-buried ancestral memories, they knew that this was somehow right, was somehow normal. And they breathed clean air for the first time in many generations.

Burl even shouted, in triumph, and his voice rang echoing among rocks. The plateau rang with the shouting of a man in triumph!

*

They had enough food for days. They had brought it from the isolated thicket not too far beneath the clouds. Had they found other food immediately, they would have settled down comfortably, in the fashion normal to creatures whose idea of bliss is a secure hiding-place and food on hand. Somehow they believed that this high place was secure. But it was not a hiding-place. And though they did accept, with the simplicity of children and savages, that they had no enemies here, their first quest, nevertheless, was for a place in which they could conceal themselves.

They found a cave. It was small to hold all of them, so that they would be crowded in it, but, as it turned out, that was fortunate.

At some time it had been occupied by some other creature, but the dirt which floored it had settled flat and there were no recent tracks. It retained faint traces of an odor which was unfamiliar but not unpleasant. It had no connotation of danger.

Ants stank of formic acid plus the musky odor of their particular city and kind. One could tell not only the kind of ant but what hill they came from, from a mere sniff at a well-traveled ant-trail. Spiders had their own hair-raising odor. The smell of a praying-mantis was acrid, and of beetles decay, and of course those bugs whose main defense was smell gave off an effluvium which tended to strangle all but themselves.

The cave's smell was quite different. The humans thought vaguely that it might be another kind of man. Actually, it *was* the smell of a warm-blooded animal. But Burl and his fellows knew of no warm-blooded creatures but themselves.

They had come above the clouds a bare two hours before sunset—of which they knew nothing. For an hour they marveled, staying close together. They were astounded by the sun, more particularly since they could not look at it. But presently, being savages, they accepted it with the matter-of-factness of children.

They could not cease to wonder at the vegetation about them. They were accustomed only to gigantic fungi, and a few feverishly growing plants striving to flower and bear seed before being devoured. Here they saw many plants, and at first no insects at all. However, they looked only for the large things they were accustomed to.

They were astounded by the slenderness of the plants. Grass fascinated them, and weeds. A large part of their courage came from the absence of debris upon the ground. In the valley, the habitation of a trapdoor spider was marked by grisly trophies—armor emptied of all meat but not yet rotted by the highly specialized bacteria which flourished upon chitin. The hunting-ground of even a mantis was marked by discarded, transparent beetle-wings and sharp spiny bits of armor, and mandibles not tasty enough to be consumed. Here, in the first hour of their exploration, they saw no sign that any insect from the lowlands had ever come to this place at all. But they interpreted the fact quite correctly as rarity, rather than complete absence of huge creatures blundering up into the sunlight.

NIGHTMARE PLANET

They were relieved that they had found a cave. There was no thicket of trees close-growing enough to shelter them. They were ludicrously amazed when they found that trees were hard and solid, because the fungi they knew were easily cut by sawtoothed tools. They found nothing to eat, but they were not yet hungry. They did not worry about it while they still had bits of edible mushroom from their climb.

When the sun sank low and the crimson colorings filled the western horizon, they shivered. They watched the glory of their first sunset with scared, incredulous eyes. Yellows and reds and purples reared toward the zenith. It became possible to look and gaze directly at the sun. They saw it descend behind something they could not guess at. Then there was dark.

The fact stunned them. So night came like this!

Then they saw the stars as they winked singly into being. And the folk from the lowland crowded frantically into the cave with its faint odor of having once been occupied. They filled the cave tightly. But Burl was somewhat reluctant to admit his fear, and Saya lingered close to him. They were the last to enter.

*

Nothing happened. Nothing. The sounds of evening continued. They were strange but infinitely soothing and somehow what night-sounds ought to be. Burl and the others could not possibly analyze it, but for the first time in many generations they were in an environment really similar to that intended for their race. It had a rightness and a goodness about it which was perceptible for all its novelty. And because Burl had once been lost from his tribe, he was capable of estimating novelties a little better than the rest.

He listened to the night-noises from close by the cave's small entrance. He heard the breathing of his tribesmen. He felt the heat of their bodies, keeping the crowded enclosure warm enough for all. Saya was close beside him. She held fast to his arm for reassurance. He was wakeful, and thinking very busily and very painfully.

Saya was filled with a tumult that was combined fear of the unknown and relief from much greater fear of the familiar ... and warm, proud memories of the sight of Burl leading and commanding the others, and memories of the look and feel of sunshine, and pictures of sky and grass and trees which she had never seen before. Emotion-filled memories of Burl as he killed a spider! Flinging a ball-fungus at a hatchling mantis, saving a young boy. Grandly leading the others up the mountainside which it had never occurred to anybody else to climb. Keeping onward sternly when it seemed that the solid ground had twisted and would drop them into a misplaced sky. And now, between her and the doorway to the strange and very beautiful night outside.

Saya felt an absorbed, impassioned, delectable disquiet from the touch of Burl's arm beneath her fingers.

He stirred. She whispered a question.

"I am going out," he murmured in her ear. "I wish to see the lights. To see if they come nearer, or move."

It had occurred to him that the first few stars they had seen glowed in darkness like the giant fireflies of the valley. They were comparable in size to all the enlarged insect kingdom. They were a yard and more in length, and sometimes at night they soared and wheeled above the lowland fungus jungles, and the segmented larval females of their kind, which never grew wings, grew frantic at the sight. They climbed recklessly upon the flat tops of toadstools and waved their dimmer twinned lanterns at the flying males.

But this was not the lowland. Burl freed his arm from Saya's fingers. He crept through the constricted opening of the cave, carrying his lance before him. He already had a vague idea that it should be not only an instrument but a weapon. He imagined stabbing enemy creatures with it—but only vaguely, as yet.

He stood upright in the open air. There was coolness. Night had fallen, but only a little while since. There were smells in the air such as Burl had never smelled before—green things growing, and the peculiar clean odor of wind that has been bathed in sunshine, and the peculiarly satisfying fragrance of coniferous trees.

But Burl raised his eyes to the heavens. He saw the stars in all their glory, and he was the first man in at least forty generations to look at them from this planet. There were myriads upon myriads of them, varying in brightness from stabbing lights to infinitesimal twinklings. They were of every possible color. They hung in the sky above him, immobile and unthreatening. They had not come nearer. They were very beautiful.

Burl stared. And then he noticed that he was breathing deeply, with a new zest. He was filling his lungs with clean, cool, fragrant air such as men were intended to breathe from the beginning, and of which Burl and many others had been deprived. It was almost intoxicating to feel so splendidly alive and unafraid.

There was a rustling. Saya stood beside him, trembling a little. To leave the others had required great courage. But she had come to realize that if any danger befell Burl she wished to share it. So she had come. They shared the starlight.

They heard the nightwind and the orchestra of night-singers. They wandered aside from the cave-mouth, and Saya found completely primitive and wholly atavistic pride in the courage of Burl, who was actually not afraid of the dark! Her own uneasiness became merely something to give more savor to her pride in him. She stayed close beside him, not only for reassurance but also for joy in being close to him.

Presently they heard a new sound in the night. It was very far away and not in the least like any sound they had ever heard before. It changed in pitch. Insect-cries do not. It was a baying, yelping sound. It rose in pitch, and held the higher note, and abruptly dropped in pitch before it ceased. Minutes later it came again.

Saya shivered, but Burl said thoughtfully:

"That is a good sound."

He didn't know why. Saya shivered once more. She said reluctantly:

"I am cold."

It had been a rare sensation in the lowlands. It came only after one of the infrequent thunderstorms, when wetted human bodies were exposed to the gusty winds that otherwise rarely blew there. But here the nights grew cold, after sundown. The heat in the ground radiated to outer space at night, not being trapped by a layer of clouds. Before dawn, the temperature would be close to freezing, though anything worse than a light fleeting hoar-frost would be rare on this plateau.

The two of them went back to the cave. It was warm there. The cave was so packed with humans that their body-heat kept the air from growing chill. Burl and Saya crouched among the rest, and became drowsy and comfortable. Presently Saya dropped off to sleep, her hand trustfully in Burl's.

But he remained awake for a long time, blinking. He thought of the stars, but they were too strange. He thought of the trees and grass. But most of the impressions of this upper world were so remote from previous knowledge that he could only accept them as they were and defer reflection upon them until later. But he did feel an enormous complacency, what with having brought his followers to an effective paradise of safety, and having arrived at a completely satisfactory emotional status with Saya.

But the last thing he actually thought about, before his eyes blinked shut in sleep, was that yelping noise he had heard in the night. It was totally novel in kind, yet there was something buried among his racial heritages that told him it was good.

*

Burl was first awake of all the tribesmen and he looked out into a cold and pallid grayness. He saw trees. One side of the cluster was brightly lighted, the other side was dark. He heard tiny singing noises of the creatures of this place. Presently he crawled out of the cave to scout for danger.

The air was biting in its chill. It was an excellent reason why giant insects could not survive here, but it was particularly invigorating as he breathed it in. Then he summoned courage to move to where he could peer at the source of this strange light.

He saw the top of the sun as it peered above the eastern cloud-bank. The sky grew lighter. He blinked at the sun and saw it rise more fully into view. He thought to look upward, and the stars that had bewildered him were nearly gone.

He ran to call Saya.

The rest of the tribe waked as he roused her. One by one they followed, to watch their first sunrise. The men and women gaped at the sun as it filled the east with colorings and rose above the seemingly steaming layer of clouds and then appeared to spring free of the horizon and swim on upward.

The children blinked and shivered and crept to their mothers for warmth. The women enclosed them in their cloaks, and they thawed and peered out once more at the glory of sunshine and the day. Soon, though, they realized that warmth came from the glaring body in the sky. The children presently discovered a game. It was the first game they had ever played, and it consisted simply of running into a shaded place until they shivered, and then of running out into the sunshine again where they were warm. Until this dawning they had never been free enough from fear to play at all. But this discovery of the nightly chill and of the utility of cloaks for warmth up here as well as it had been against the nightly rain of the lowlands, was a specific suggestion of the value of clothing. Which was to have another significance, a short time later.

In this first dawn of their experience, the tribesmen ate of the edible mushroom they had brought up the mountain-flank. But there was not an indefinite amount of food left. Burl shared the meal Saya brought him. She touched him fondly. But he regarded his happy fellows with something like a scowl. They were quite contented, and they had for the moment no need of his guidance. They did not look to him for orders. And Burl wanted attention.

He spoke abruptly.

"We do not want to go back to the place we came from," he said sternly. "We must look for food here, so we can stay for always. Today we look for food."

It was a seizure of the initiative. It was the linking of what the folk most craved with obedience to Burl. It was the instinct of a leader. The eating men murmured agreement. There was a certain definite idea of goodness—not moral virtue, but of the desirable—becoming associated with what Burl did and what Burl commanded. His tribe was becoming a group of which he was the leader, rather than only a loose association held together only by the fear of solitude.

He led them exploring as soon as they had eaten. All of them, of course. None had yet become confident enough to be left behind. They straggled irregularly behind Burl and Saya. They came to a brook and regarded it with amazement. There were no leeches. No fungus. No swiftly drifting islands of scum. It was clear. Greatly daring, Burl tasted it and it was water, but such as he had never tasted before. It was clean, fresh, sparkling water, not fouled by drainage through mould or rust.

The rest of the tribe tasted. A child slipped on a muddy place and sat down hard on white stuff that yielded and almost splashed. The child howled. Saya picked it up. Then she looked where it had been for spines or small stinging things.

She stared blankly.

She went to Burl with a tiny white thing in her hand. It was a mushroom. But it was a *tiny*, clean, appetizing object. Saya had no words for it. She was amazed.

Burl smelled it carefully. He tasted it. And it was actually no more and no less than a normal mushroom, growing in a shaded place upon enormously rich soil. It had been protected from sunlight, but it had not the means nor the stimulus to become a monster.

Burl ate it. He carefully composed his features. Then he announced the find to his followers.

There was food here, he told them. But in this splendid world to which he had led them, food was small. There would be no great enemies here, but the food would have to be sought in small objects rather than great ones. They must look at this place and seek others like it, where food would be found....

The tribesmen were doubtful. But they plucked mushrooms—whole ones!—instead of merely breaking off parts of their tops. In deep astonishment they recognized miniatures of what they had known only in gigantic forms. They tasted. The tiny mushrooms had the same savor, but they were not coarse or stringy or tough like the giants. They melted in the mouth! Life in this place to which Burl had led them was delectable! Truly the doings of Burl were astonishing!

When a child found a beetle on a leaf, and they recognized it, they were entranced, for instead of being bigger than a man and a thing to flee from, it was less than an inch in size and helpless against them. From that moment on, they would follow Burl anywhere and obey him in any matter, in the happy conviction that he could do nothing that was not desirable in all respects.

The belief, of course, was not quite accurate. Tender tiny mushrooms as a staple, instead of the tough and chewy provender they were used to, in time would cause them to have toothaches. But they could not anticipate it, and it was actually very far away in time.

They struggled after Burl through vast patches of bushes with thorns on them. They were not used to thorns, and they deeply distrusted the bushes and even the glistening fruit on them, which eventually they would know were blackberries. Near midday they heard noises in the distance.

The sounds were made up of cries of varying pitch, some of which were sharp and abrupt, and others longer and less loud. The people did not understand them in the least. They could have been the cries of human beings, but they were assuredly not cries of pain. Also they were not language. They seemed to convey an impression of enormous, zestful excitement. They had no overtone of horror. And Burl and his folk had known of no excitement among insects except the frenzy of ferocity. They were unable to imagine even the nature of the tumult.

To Burl the cries seemed to have somewhat the timbre of the yelping sounds he had heard the night before. And he had felt instinctively drawn to that sound. He liked it.

He led the way boldly in the direction of the noise. And presently he came out of breast-high weeds with Saya close behind him and the others trailing. He emerged upon a space of bare stone, a little upraised. He looked down into a small and grassy amphitheater. The tumult came from its center.

A pack of dogs were joyously attacking something that Burl could not see clearly. They *were dogs*. They barked zestfully, and they yelped and snarled and yapped in a dozen different voices, and they darted at the unseen something and darted away, and they were having a thoroughly enjoyable time, though it might not be so good for the thing they attacked.

One of them saw the humans and stopped stock-still and barked. The others whirled and saw the humans as they came out into view. The tumult ceased entirely.

There was silence. The men for the first time saw creatures with only four legs. They had never before seen any moving thing with fewer than six—except men. Spiders had eight. The dogs did not have mandibles. They did not act like insects.

And the dogs saw men, whom they had never seen before. Much more important, they smelled men. And the difference between man-smell and that of insects was vast. Through many generations the dogs had not smelled anything with warm blood save their own kind. The difference in smell between insect and man was so great that the dogs did not react with suspicion, but with curiosity. This was an unparalleled smell. It was even a good smell.

The dogs regarded the men with their heads on one side, sniffing them in the deepest possible amazement—amazement so intense that they could not feel hostility. One of them whined a little because he did not understand.

*

Peculiarly enough, it was a matter of topography. The plateau which reached above the clouds rose with a steep slope from the valley in which Burl and the others had lived. To westward, however, the highland was subject to an indentation which almost severed it. No more than twenty miles from where Burl's group had climbed to sunshine, there was a much more gradual slope downward. There, mushroom-forests grew almost to the cloud-layer. From there, giant insects strayed up and onto the plateau itself. They could not live on the plateau, of course. There was no food for their insatiable hunger. Especially at night, there was no warmth to keep them active. But they did stray from their normal environment, and some of them reached the sunshine, and perhaps some of them blundered back down to their mushroom-forests again. But those that did not find their way back were chilled to torpor during their first night on the highland. They were only partly active on the second day if, indeed, they were active at all. And few or none recovered from the second night of cold. Certainly none kept their full ferocity and deadliness. And this was how the dogs survived.

Unquestionably the dogs were descended from dogs on the wrecked ship—name now unknown—which had landed on this planet some forty-odd human generations since. The humans had no memories of that ship, and the dogs had surely no traditions. But perhaps because those early dogs had less of intellect, they had possessed more useful instincts. Perhaps dogs were bred by the first desperate generations of humans, to warn them against dangers. But no human civilization could survive the environment of the lowlands. The humans inevitably reverted to the primitive. The environment was not one in which dogs could survive, so somehow they took to the heights. Perhaps dogs survived their masters. Perhaps some were abandoned or driven away. But dogs had reached the heights. And they did survive because of the simple fact that giant insects blundered up after them—and could not survive the proper environment for dogs and men.

There was even a reason why they had not multiplied excessively. The food-supply was limited. When there were too many dogs, their attacks on stumbling insects were more desperate, and made earlier before ferocity of the insects was lessened. And more dogs died. So there was a specific adjustment of the dog population to the food-supply. There was also a selection of those intelligent enough not to attack foolishly, but not of those whose cowardice left them out of conflict altogether.

These dogs who regarded men with their heads cocked on one side were excellent dogs. Intelligent dogs. They did not attack anything imprudently, and they knew it was not necessary to be more than wary of insects in general. Even spiders, unless they were very newly arrived from the lowlands. So the attitude of men and dogs was that of astonished curiosity rather than that of instant fear or rage. Burl knew that the shaggy, bright-eyed creatures were unlike insects. Actually, they behaved strikingly like men. They were estimating these strange beings, men. Insects never estimated. Those that were not carnivorous had no interest in anything but food, and those that were carnivorous lumbered insanely into battle the instant any prey came to their notice. The dogs did neither. They sniffed. They considered. They were amazed.

Burl said harshly to his group:

"Stay here!"

He walked slowly down into the amphitheater. Saya, disregarding his order, followed him instantly. The dogs moved warily aside. But they raised their noses and sniffed—long, luxurious sniffs. The smell of humankind was a good smell. Dogs had gone hundreds of generations without having it in their nostrils. But before that there were thousands of generations of dogs to whom that smell was a fulfillment.

Burl reached the object the dogs had been attacking. It lay on the grass, throbbing painfully. It had come up from the world below. It was the larva of an azure-blue moth which spread ten-foot wings at nightfall. The time for its metamorphosis was near, and it had gone blindly in search of a place where it could spin its cocoon safely and change to its winged form. It had come to another world—the world above the clouds. It could find no proper place. Its stores of fat had protected it a little from the chill. But the dogs had found it.

Burl considered. It was the custom of wasps to sting creatures like this within a certain special spot—marked for them apparently by a tuft of dark fur.

Burl thrust his lance into that particular spot. The creature died quickly and without agony. The thought to kill was an inspiration, which was the result of continued adventuring. Burl cut off meat for his tribesmen. The dogs offered no objection. They were well-fed enough. Burl and Saya, together, carried the meat back to the blinking tribesfolk. On the way they passed within two yards of a dog which regarded them with extreme intent and almost a wistful expression. Their smell did not mean game. It meant—something the dog struggled dumbly to remember.

"I have killed the thing," said Burl, in the tone of one speaking to an equal. "You can go and eat it now. I took only part of it."

The dog wagged its tail—and then backed away as if in confusion. After all, matters had not yet progressed to cordiality.

The humans consumed what Burl had brought them. Most of the dogs went to the feast Burl had left. Presently they were back. They had no reason to be hostile. They were fed. The humans offered them no injury. The humans smelled good. The dogs were fascinated by their smell.

Presently they were close about the humans. They were not insects. They were interested. The humans were extremely interested in anything which was interested in them. It was a wholly novel experience. It was the feeling Burl had felt in becoming the tribal leader. Now every human felt a little of it, in the intent regard of the dogs. And everything else was so strange that it was possible to accept anything without question. Even the possible friendliness of unparalleled creatures which assuredly were not of a kind with past enemies.

A similar state of "mind" existed among the dogs.

Saya had more meat than she desired. She looked about among the humans. All were well supplied. She tossed it to a dog. He jerked away alertly, and then sniffed at the meat where it had dropped. A dog can always eat. He ate it.

"I wish you would talk to us," said Saya hopefully.

The dog wagged his tail.

"You do not look like us," said Saya interestedly, "but you act as we do. Not as the—monsters!"

The dog looked at meat in Burl's hand. Burl tossed it. The dog caught it with a quick snap, swallowed it, wagged his tail briefly and came closer. It was a completely incredible action, but dogs and men were blood-kin on this planet. Besides, there was subconscious racial-memory instinct in friendship between man and dog. It was not overlaid by any past experience of either. They were the only warm-blooded creatures on this world. It was kinship felt by both.

Burl stood up and spoke politely to the dog. He addressed him with the same respect he would have given to another man. In all his life he had never felt equal to an insect, but he felt no arrogance toward this dog.

He felt superior only to other men.

"We are going back to our cave," he said politely. "Maybe we will meet again."

He led his tribe back to the cave in which they had spent the previous night. The dogs followed, ranging on either side. They were well-fed, with no memory of hostility to any creature which smelled like men. They had instinct and intelligence. The latter part of the return to the cave—if anybody had been qualified to notice—was remarkably like a group of dogs taking a walk with a group of people. It was companionable. It felt remarkably right.

That night Burl left the cave, as before, to look at the stars. This time Saya went with him, gladly. But as they emerged from the cave-entrance there was a stirring. A dog rose and stretched itself elaborately, yawning the while. When Burl and Saya walked aside from the cave, the dog trotted amiably with them.

They talked to it, embarrassed. And the dog seemed pleased. It wagged its tail.

When morning came the dogs were still waiting hopefully for the humans to come out. They appeared to expect the humans to take another nice long walk, on which they would accompany them. It was a brand-new satisfaction they did not wish to miss. After all, from a dog's standpoint, humans were made to take long walks with, among other things. The dogs greeted the humans with tail-waggings and cordiality.

*

The friendship of the dogs assured the humans' new status in life. They had ceased to be fugitive game for any insect murderer. They had hoped to be unpursued foragers. But, joined to the dogs, they were raised to the estate of hunters. The men did not domesticate the dogs. They made friends with them. The dogs did not subjugate themselves to the men.

They joined them, at first tentatively and then with worshipful enthusiasm. And the partnership was so inherently right that within a month it was as if it had been always. And indeed, except for a few centuries, for them, it had.

The humans had made a permanent encampment by then. There were a few caves at an appropriate distance from the slope up which most wanderers from the lowlands came. The humans moved into the caves. A child found the chrysalis of a giant butterfly, whose caterpillar form had so offensive an odor that the dogs had not attacked it. But when it emerged from the chrysalis, humans and dogs together assailed it before it could take flight. They ended with warm approval of each other. The humans had great wings with which to make cloaks. And men wore cloaks now—shorter than the women's—but cloaks. They were very useful against the evening chill. When one dawning a vast outcry of dogs awoke the humans, Burl led the rush to the spot, and his great lance did execution which the dogs appeared to admire. Burl wore a moth's feathery antennae, now, bound to his forehead like a knight's plumes. They were very splendid.

In a single month their entire way of life went through a revolution. The ground was often thorny. A man pierced his foot, and bandaged it with a strip of wing-fabric so he could walk. The injured foot was more comfortable to walk with than the well one. Within a week women were busily contriving divers forms of footgear, to achieve the greatest comfort. One day Saya admired glistening red berries and tried to pluck them, and they stained her fingers. She licked the fingers—and berries were added to the tribe's menu. A veritable orgy of experimentation began. And this was a state of affairs which is very, very rare among human beings. A tribe with an established culture and tradition cannot change without disaster. But men who have abandoned their old ways and are seeking new ones can go far.

Already the dogs were established as sentries and watchmen and friends to every one of the humans. By now mothers did not feel alarmed if a child wandered out of sight. There would be dogs along. No danger could approach a child without vociferous warning from the dogs. Men went hunting, now, with zestful tail-wagging dogs as companions in the chase. By the time a stray monster from the lowlands reached this area, it was dazed and half-numbed by at least one night of bitter cold. Even spiders could not find energy to leap. They fought like fiends, but sluggishly. Men could kill them while dogs kept their attention. Burl killed one the third week on the plateau. He was nerved to the deed by a peculiar feeling that he must be worthy of the courage of the dogs with him at the time.

And presently, while their way of life was still fluid, the permanent pattern of civilization on the nightmare planet was settled. Burl and Saya went out early one morning with the dogs, to hunt for meat for the village. Hunting was easiest in the morning while creatures strayed up the night before were still numbed. Often, hunting was merely butchery of an enfeebled monster to whom any sort of movement was enormous effort.

This morning the humans moved briskly. The dogs roamed exuberantly through the brush before them. They were five miles from the village when the dogs bayed game some distance ahead. And Burl and Saya ran to the spot hand in hand—which was something of a change from their former actions at the thought of a giant creature of the insect kind—and found the dogs dancing and barking around one of the most ferocious and most ghastly of the carnivorous beetles. It was not too large, to be sure. Its body might have been four feet long, but its horrid mandibles added three feet more.

Those scythe-like objects gaped wide—opening sidewise as a beetle's jaws do—and snapped hideously, swinging about as the dogs dashed at them. The legs were spurred and spiked and armed with dagger-like spines. Burl plunged into the fight.

The great gaping mandibles clicked and clashed. They were capable of disemboweling a man or snapping a dog's body in half without effort. There were whistling noises as the beetle breathed through its abdominal spiracles. It fought furiously, making frantic plunges at the dogs who dashed in and out to torment and bewilder it while they created the most zestfully excited of uproars.

There was something beside this conflict that Burl and Saya should have noticed, but they were instantly intent. The other thing was quite unparalleled. There had been nothing else like it on this planet in many hundreds of years. It moved slowly above the plateau as if examining it. It was half a dozen miles away and perhaps a mile higher when Burl and Saya prepared to intervene professionally on behalf of the dogs. Then it swerved and moved directly toward them. It moved swiftly.

But it was silent, and they did not know at all. Burl leaped in with a lance-thrust at the tough integument where an armored leg joined the body. He missed, and the monster whirled. Then Saya flashed her cloak before the beetle, so that it seemed a larger and nearer antagonist. As the creature whirled again, Burl thrust once more and a hind-leg crumpled.

Instantly the thing limped crazily. A beetle does not use its legs like four-legged creatures. It moves the two end legs on one side with the center leg on the other, so that always it is braced on an adjustable tripod. But it cannot adjust readily to crippling.

A dog snatched at a spiny lower leg and crunched and darted away. The expressionless, machine-like horror uttered a formless, deep-bass cry and was spurred to all possible ferocity. The fight became a thing of furious movement and uproar, with Burl striking once at a multiple eye so the pain would deflect it from a charge on Saya, and Saya again deflecting it with her cloak and once breathlessly trying to strike it with her shorter spear.

Then the beetle sank to the ground, all three legs on one side crippled. The remaining three thrust and thrust and struggled terribly and suddenly it was on its back, still striking its gigantic jaws frantically in the hope of murder. But Burl stabbed home between two armor-plates where a ganglion was almost exposed. A thrust killed it instantly.

Burl and Saya smiled at each other. There was a monstrous sound of splintering trees. They whirled. The dogs pricked up their ears. One of them barked defiantly.

*

Something huge—truly huge!—settled to the ground a bare hundred yards away. It was metal, and there were ports, and it was utterly beyond experience, because, of course, there had been no spaceship landings on this planet in forty-odd human generations. But as Burl and Saya stared blankly at it, a port opened, and men came out, and they waved hopefully to the two barbarically attired figures who had been seen fighting a monster with the help of dogs. Which meant some sort of civilization.

The dogs confirmed it. They sniffed. These, also, were men. And Burl and his tribe had this smell, and were friends. So the dogs trotted forward with the self-confident cordiality of dogs on excellent terms with men—and there was no question of friendship. None at all. The men came forward

41

joyously to talk to Burl and Saya.

There were difficulties, of course. But Burl and Saya had the calm composure of savages, and the alertness of people who are changing the pattern of their lives of their own volition—and finding it very pleasant—and things went swimmingly. There was, on the spaceship, an "educator." They invited Burl to put it on his head. He obliged. And very shortly he understood a new language, and was equipped with a very considerable fund of general information. Among the items of information was the fact that presently he would have a splitting headache—he did—and that the making of records for an educator was so different that it required generations to get all the facts and knowledge for a single type of education down in permanent form.

All of which fitted admirably into the arrangements that the men on the spaceship were anxious to make, and Burl was enthusiastically willing to accede to. He and his folk knew the creatures of the lowlands as nobody else could possibly know them. No electronic educator could possibly make a record making available that knowledge in less than two generations—maybe three. Therefore—

*

The nightmare world swims in space about its nearby sun. It has a name now, but it does not matter. It has a city on it, which probably matters less. It is a curious city, though. The people in it wear gorgeous colored fur, and cloaks of butterfly wings. The least of the people in that city wear garments which would fetch fortunes on other inhabited worlds. In fact, such garments do. But it is most practical for Burl, and Saya, and their followers to wear such garments. There is no day but that a small, winged flying craft rises from the city to go silently over the plateau until it reaches the space above the cloud-bank, and then dives down into it. It is wise for the occupants and the operators of such small craft to wear garments like the other humans on this planet. They are recognized, that way, when garments such as most planets find suitable would make them seem strange.

They want to be recognized, in the jungles and the noisesome valleys of the lowlands. There are other humans down there. The people of the city, of course, bring their fellows out as fast as they can find them. There is a session with an educator—and a splitting headache afterward—and very soon the folk who have hidden from monsters all their lives are zestfully hunting them with dogs. Presently they are hunting them with flying machines.

It is a nice arrangement. The search for more people in the lowlands is a prosperous business even when it is unsuccessful. The wings of white morph butterflies bring the highest price, but even a common swallow-tail is riches enough. And the fur of caterpillars—duly processed—goes into the holds of the regular spaceliners with the same care given elsewhere to jewels and platinum.

But the nightmare planet has not become a merely sordid place of business. What comforts and what luxuries spaceships can bring are available enough, to be sure. But the city on the plateau, and the homes of the barbarically clad inhabitants are not places to which invitations are coveted for the luxury of them. The planet is a sportman's paradise.

Not long since, the Planet President of *Surmor III* was a guest in Burl's dwelling. Burl is all hard muscle, despite his graying hair, and he and Saya have fitted very beautifully into the sort of civilization that turned out to be congenial to them. They have grown children now, and their home is quite fit to entertain a World President in its richness. But it is small—the size they want it to be.

The atmosphere is oddly informal. There are self-respecting and amiable dogs nearly everywhere. The World President of *Surmor III* was inclined to be stand-offish at first. But he is a sportsman, like Burl. And since the last hunting trip, he is very respectful. After all, there are few planet leaders who will, as they do, for pure sporting joy of the hunt, fight the mastodon-sized tarantula of the lowlands with nothing but a spear—and win.

But Burl does.

www.ingramcontent.com/pod-product-compliance
Lightning Source LLC
Chambersburg PA
CBHW050917120626
46552CB00004B/1612